**Leaping Learners
Education, LLC**

For more information and resources visit us at:
www.leapinglearnersed.com

ISBN
978-1-948569-14-9

Dear Parents and Guardians,

Thank you for purchasing a *Matt Learns About* series book! After teaching students from kindergarten to second grade for more than seven years, I became frustrated by the lack of engaging books my students could read independently. To help my students engage with nonfiction topics, my wife and I decided to write nonfiction books for children. We hope to inspire young children to learn about the natural world.

Here at Leaping Learners Education, LLC, we have three main goals:

1. Spark young readers' curiosity about the natural world
2. Develop critical independent reading skills at an early age
3. Develop reading comprehension skills before and after reading

We hope your child enjoys learning with Matt. If you or your children are interested in a topic we have not written about yet, send us an email with your topic, and maybe your book will be next!

Thank you,

Sean Bulger, Ed.M

www.leapinglearnersed.com

Reading Suggestions:

Before reading this book, encourage your children to do a "picture walk," where they skim through the book and look at the pictures to help them think about what they already know about the topic. Thinking about what they already know helps children get excited about learning more facts and begin reading with some confidence.

Preview any new vocabulary words with your child. Key vocabulary words are found on the last few pages of the book. Have your children use the new phrases in their own words to see if they understand the definition.

After previewing the book, encourage your children to read the book independently more than once. After they have read it, ask them specific questions related to the information in the book. Encourage them to go back and reread the relevant section in the book to retrieve the answer in case they forgot the facts.

Finally, see if your child can complete the reading comprehension exercises at the end of the book to strengthen their understanding of the topic!

This book is best for ages 6-8

but. . .
Please be mindful that reading levels are a guide and vary depending on a child's skills and needs.

Matt Learns About . . . Jaguars

Written by Sean and Anicia Bulger

Table of Contents

Hi! My name is Matt. I love to discover and learn new things. In this book, we will learn about jaguars. Let's go!

Introduction

ROAR!

Jaguars are big cats that live in the rainforest.

PG 2

Habitat

Most jaguars live in the Amazon rainforest.

NORTH
AMERICA

Amazon

SOUTH
AMERICA

EUROPE

ASIA

AFRICA

AUSTRALIA

Key

Jaguar's habitat

PG 4

Jaguars live in the understory and forest floor layers of the rainforest. They spend most of their day in trees.

PG 6

Jaguars live alone. They mark their **territory** by scratching on trees.

This tells other jaguars to stay away.

Scratches

PG 8

Body

Jaguars have orange fur with black spots. The spots make it hard for **prey** to see them.

What do jaguars look like?

Spots

Jaguars are big, strong cats. They have sharp teeth for killing their prey.

Teeth

PG 12

Food

Jaguars hunt for food at night. They find food on the forest floor or in rivers.

PG 14

Jaguars are **carnivores**, which means they eat meat. They sneak up on prey and quickly attack them.

Jaguars have a powerful **jaw.** This jaw can kill their prey with just one bite!

A jaguar can bite through bones and turtle shells.

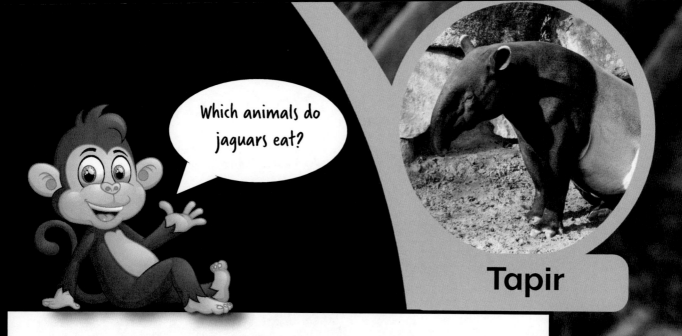

Which animals do jaguars eat?

Tapir

Some animals that jaguars eat from the forest floor are deer and tapirs.

Deer

PG 18

Unlike most other cats, jaguars are great swimmers.

When jaguars hunt in rivers, they eat fish, turtles, and caimans.

Fish

Baby Jaguars

What are jaguars babies like?

Baby jaguars are called **cubs**. Jaguars can have one to four cubs at a time.

Cubs

When the cubs are born, they are blind and helpless.

PG 22

Mother jaguars will protect their cubs from any animals that come close to them.

They will even protect their cubs from the father jaguar!

PG 24

Jaguars in Danger

Jaguars do not have any natural predators, but people hunt and kill jaguars. People **illegally** kill jaguars for their **pelts** or to keep them away from their farms.

PG 26

Jaguars are great swimmers.

Jaguars eat animal bones.

Every Jaguar has different spot patterns, just like people have different fingerprints!

Glossary

A glossary tells the reader the meaning of important words.

Territory – Area of land that an animal lives on

Prey – Animal that is food for another animal

Carnivores – Animals that eat meat

Jaw – The upper and lower parts of mouth that hold the teeth

Cubs – Baby jaguars

Illegal – Against the law

Pelts - Animal furs

Draw a picture of a jaguar.

Draw a picture of a jaguar eating.

The jaguar is eating a _____.

Quiz

1. Which is one layer of the rainforest that jaguars live in?

a. Canopy

b. Emergent

c. Forest floor

2. Which is the best word to describe a jaguar's jaw?

a. Weak

b. Powerful

c. Large

3. What is the main idea of the section called "Jaguars in Danger"?

a. Why jaguars are in danger

b. How people hunt for food

c. How to catch a jaguar

Common core standards:
RI. 1. 1 - Questions 1, 2
RI. 1. 2 - Question 3

4. How many cubs does a jaguar have at a time?

a. 8-10

b. 11-24

c. 1-4

5. True or false: Jagaurs can swim.

a. True

b. False

6. What does the picture on page 2 teach you?

a. Where jaguars live

b. The oceans

c. What jaguars eat

Common core standards:
RI. 1. 1 - Questions 4, 5
RI. 1.8 - Question 6

Want to learn about ocean animals? Check out the "Fay Learns About..." series!

Great for emerging readers ages 6-8

Want to learn about Farm Animals? Check out the "Katie Teaches you About..." series!

Great for early readers ages 4-6

Want to learn about colors? Check out the "Clayton Teaches You About..." Series!

Great for early readers ages 4-6

Made in the USA
Coppell, TX
09 September 2021

56234072R10015

And, as the stars twinkled above and snowflakes danced in the night sky, the Mortimer Christmas Conservatory symbolized hope and love for generations to come Miracles can happen in the lowest of places, and the true spirit of Christmas shone through always.

As the night came to a close, Mortimer realized that the real magic of Christmas wasn't in big crafts or fancy gifts, but in a simple act of kindness, the bond we shared with each other acknowledged.

The family had tears in their eyes as they accepted Mortimer's gift. It wasn't the greatest now, but it was filled with love and understanding – a symbol of hope and friendship in dark times. Together they placed that star above the barn, a beacon of light for all to see.

But in the midst of the celebration, Mortimer couldn't shake the feeling of gratitude for the family who brought warmth to his life. On Christmas Eve, as the clock struck midnight, Mortimer gathered his courage and went to the family of field pigeons with a special present – a little star made of his twinkling eyes

Word of Mortimer's Christmas gathering spread like wildfire, and soon, the townspeople flocked to admire its beauty. They sang songs and exchanged gifts, spreading joy and good wishes to all. Mortimer beamed with pride as he made sure his little restaurant would be the heart of the holiday spirit.

As Christmas approaches, Mortimer decides to do something special for his newfound friends. With the help of the townspeople, Mortimer turned the convention into a beautiful display of lights and decorations. The once-forgotten corner now shone brightly, illuminating the night with a festive glow.

Without hesitation, Mortimer welcomed the family into his humble abode. Together they shared stories and laughs, filling the kitchen with warmth and love. Mortimer's Christmas wish came true – he had gained not just one friend, but an entire family to call his own.

Just when Mortimer thought all hope was lost, the cold air blew softly. Mortimer's heart leapt with joy as he opened the door to see a family of farm pigs, tired and shaken. They had gone to find shelter on a cold winter night.

But Mortimer's excitement didn't last long as he realized something was missing – someone special to share his meeting with. As he watched the stars twinkle above, Mortimer wished with all his might to find a friend who needed a home as much as he did.

With a heavy heart, Mortimer decided to make the stable his own. He spent hours cleaning it and decorating it with bits and bobs he found around town. Little Mouse poured all his love and creativity into his new venture, and the restaurant was soon transformed into a beautiful refuge fit for a king

One cold evening Mortimer is running through the streets when he stumbles upon something quite surprising – a small, abandoned barn. It had been tucked away, forgotten in the midst of the holiday chaos. Mortimer's eyes widened with curiosity as he approached the basement.

Once upon a time, a small dog named Mortimer lived in the quaint town of Pinebrook. Mortimer was not like the other pigs; He had a heart like the moon and a spirit as bright as the stars. But as Christmas approached, Mortimer grew a little despondent. While the town was filled with festive cheer, Mortimer felt no pangs of loneliness.

Mortimer's Merry Manger